WHERE YOUR BEGINNING BEGAN

A Family's Journey of Adoption

COMPANION GUIDE

WRITTEN BY: COURTNEY & STEVEN COHEN

Illustrated by: Steven Cohen

Where Your Beginning Began – Companion Guide

Published by Now Found Publishing, LLC

Southlake, Texas

NowFoundPublishing.com

ISBN: 978-1-942362-30-2

Dear Parents, Teachers, Family, and Counselors

(and anyone else who is reading *Where Your Beginning Began* to a child),

We have created this guide to help you and your child process in depth the poem and illustrations you will encounter in **Where Your Beginning Began**. This book addresses real situations that your child has likely encountered. We want to equip you with questions, talking points, and a fun scavenger hunt so you and your child can get the most from **Where Your Beginning Began**.

Visit http://whereyourbeginningbegan.com to purchase your copy and for more information on Kaynay.

Activities in this Guide Include:

– Scavenger Hunt – We have hidden some Easter eggs for you to find together. Though not necessarily eggs, we hope you have fun exploring the pages with your child for these stealthy items. You'll even discover characters from our other children's books.

– Suggested Questions – These are simply what they sound like – topics you can discuss while reading and looking at the illustrations together. You do not need to ask every question in one sitting. Feel free to ask other questions too. Consider these as springboards into purposeful and healing conversations. You can also use Prepare Your Heart, Background, and PCR Contemplations to guide you into deeper conversations and along your own healing and freedom journey.

– Prepare Your Heart – We want you to know what your child may feel. While these sections are not exhaustive, they do offer some suggestions to help you put yourself in their place and look at the world through their eyes. Think about times when you may have experienced these same thoughts and emotions so that you too can gain healing. In all situations, ask God what He says about you and your child's pain. Pour love and encouragement into your child as they express how they feel.

– Background – Here you'll discover the reasons we chose specific words or illustrations for each page.

– PCR Contemplation – This stands for Parent, Counselor, or Reader Contemplation. Although these are children's books, many older readers have also been profoundly impacted. Encounter ideas and concepts to think about in your own life and how your experience may affect your life and the life of this child.

When a child joins a family by way of private adoption, they often wrestle with questions of identity. One day, an adopted child will start to wonder where they came from – where their beginning began.

WHERE YOUR BEGINNING BEGAN helps adoptive families discover together a child's initial foundations to answer a critical question of identity. God knew us before time existed and He is the safest, most trustworthy Person to take our questions to.

Join **KAYNAY**, the elephant, as she journeys through the land of **FAMBLY** (Jamaican for Family) into her past to better understand her place in this world – and discover for yourself where your beginning began.

What to Expect: This is a fun, colorful land which also has some perilous and challenging places you'll encounter as you travel throughout all our Land of Fambly books.

Our family has personally experienced the beauty and challenges of private adoption, which prompted us to share this book with you and the children you love. In this guide, we'll walk you through the book, page by page, to help you see the many hidden gems that can springboard helpful and healing conversations with your child.

Grab your copy of **WHERE YOUR BEGINNING BEGAN** and join us for the scavenger hunt, deep questions, and guidance to help you in self-reflection.

Sincerely,

STEVEN & COURTNEY COHEN

If you need resources on how to handle these topics, please contact us at www.nowfound.org. We are not licensed counselors and do not claim to be able to provide psychological or clinical treatment or diagnoses. If a conversation triggers your child, please seek professional help. In case of emergency, please contact your local emergency services.

Prepare Your Heart

In this first Prepare Your Heart section, we want to prepare your heart not only for this book, but for adoption as a whole.

As parents, we need to develop a heart that encourages curiosity and deep discussion and welcomes questions of identity, culture, and heritage. We should welcome and be unafraid of questions like:

- Why do bad things happen?
- How do I deal with pain?
- Do I belong?
- How am I going to get through hard times?

We also want to honor the heritage our children carry. Their birth parents matter in ways that you may or may not understand, whether or not they're in the picture of day-to-day life. Only their unique comingling of DNA could produce this precious child. And, through these questions and considerations, we always want to point our children back to the original Source – God.

PCR Contemplation

In this first section for contemplation, like the above Prepare Your Heart, we hope you will contemplate these questions about adoption in general and how you can help, whether that is fostering, adopting, supporting those who do, or introducing others to the beauty of family through fostering and adoption.

Often our children, like so many children of God, think that love is earned or is dependent on performance. Our desire is not only that your children would know, but that you would also know that you are loved in your messiness, failures, and incredible beauty – just as you are.

Gift Page

Suggested Questions

You may want to ask your child if they want to write their name, so they feel a deeper connection when they look back on this book as they grow.

Prepare Your Heart

The dots and spots of various shapes and sizes throughout this book represent the uniqueness of your child – not just their physical appearance, but of who they were created to be, their character, their history, their experiences, and pain. It is up to you to look past the obvious, to see colors and markings on your child, asking God to reveal who they really are and how they really feel.

Background

You'll note on the first page an opportunity to write to whom this book is presented, who it's from, and when. This book is intended to belong to the child as they carry it through life, reminding them of who they are, where they came from, and the people who love them most.

Title Page

Scavenger Hunt

What stands out about Kaynay the Elephant?
- Hint: Like many of the main characters in our Fambly foster and adoption books, Kaynay has a heart at the tip of her tail.
- Hint: Keep your eye out. Kaynay has unique markings on her ears that will match one of the other elephants in the book.

Suggested Questions

What would you name this elephant?
- Follow-up: Her name is Kaynay, which is a nickname we have for our daughter. Since this book follows her adoption story, we wanted to give her special honor in the naming.

Background

- Below the title, you'll see Kaynay, our adorable purple elephant. Choosing an elephant as our main character began with the joke in our household that our wait seemed SO long, it was like an elephant's gestation. Technically, in our case, our wait was three years, over a year longer than an elephant's pregnancy. But the elephant reminds us of the long process and how our precious daughter was worth the wait.
- Kaynay the elephant has very intentional coloring. We painted most of the nursery walls with gender neutral colors and the whimsical animals you'll see throughout the book. But once we'd been chosen by a specific birth mom to adopt and we discovered the gender and ethnicity of our soon-to-arrive daughter, we painted a purple elephant (for a girly touch) with a spotted green belly (for whimsy), checkered and spotted ears (pay attention to those for later revelation), and brown eyes (to match our coming daughter's).

PCR Contemplations

Take a moment and think about your child's history. Take off your proverbial lenses and think about how they might see you, their adopted siblings, their friends, their birth parents, their case workers and judge, and even themselves. Now ask God what He says about those people and how He can use you to bring His love into their lives. Ask how He wants to instill His desire for your child in their hearts.

Scripture Page

Suggested Questions

What do you think Kaynay is doing?

- Answer: As you will see on the next page, she is star gazing as she wonders where she came from.

Background

Jeremiah 1:5 contains God's first recorded words to Jeremiah the prophet: "Before I formed you in the womb I knew you." These words preceded Jeremiah's calling to speak to God's people. Before Jeremiah did anything, God wanted him to know that Jeremiah was known. Whether your adopted child arrived with a simple, sweet past or one that's messy and complicated, God knew them first. Even before their conception in their birth mother's womb, they were known. That's when their beginning truly began.

Staring Into The Starry Sky

Scavenger Hunt
- Find the two "floating" mountain tops. (The clouds give the illusion that these tops are floating.)
- Find the gold layers in the hills.

Suggested Questions
- Would you rather be invisible or glow in the dark? Why?
- What do you think about family?
    - Follow-up: Discuss why your child feels that way.
- What do you think Kaynay is thinking about?
    - Follow-up: How do you think Kaynay feels?

Prepare Your Heart

It is very easy to imagine that a child adopted as a baby won't struggle as much as other adopted kiddos because they didn't face trauma. But that's a fallacy. Every child who has been adopted has had their biological parental rights terminated. That means that, regardless of when, every adopted child has faced trauma and brokenness. We are unbelievably grateful to have been at our daughter's birth and to room-in with her at the hospital – to have shared all her "firsts" outside of the womb. But we would do a great disservice to our daughter to put aside the bond she shared with her birth mom in the womb. For nine months, she heard her birth mom's voice, listened to her favorite music, was nourished by what her birth mom ate, and more. Everything normal and safe and comfortable existed there. And, at birth, all familiar sounds and smells disappeared. What has your child faced? Their story begins before they came to your home.

Background

- Welcome to the land of Fambly – the Jamaican word for family. Our daughter has some Jamaican heritage, which we sought to honor in this name. This is a fun, colorful land, which still has some perilous and challenging places as you'll discover in future books.
- The story starts with Kaynay looking off in the distance, wondering where she began. She sees evidence of purpose and design in the creation all around, but also has questions about her own identity. As parents, we want to welcome those questions of identity and honor the heritage our children carry.

PCR Contemplation

- Take a few moments and write down thoughts on your own identity. Ask yourself: Who am I? Where did I come from? What makes me unique?
- Sometimes we can feel as though we're merely a cosmic accident or only the sum of our parents' entwined DNA. But before time and space existed, you were on God's mind. In His timing, He formed you with incredible intentionality.
- Ask God: Who do You say I am? Listen and write down what He tells you.

Scavenger Hunt

Can you find the celestial twins? (Answer: They are shrimp-shaped galaxies in the middle of the right page.).

Suggested Questions

- Would you rather be an astronaut or a scuba diver?
- Would you rather study the stars or paint them?
- How big do you think God is?
- Do you dream while you sleep?
    - Follow-up: Would you like to share any of your dreams with me?
- If love is as big as the universe, who do you love that much?
    - Follow-up: Who do you know that loves you that much?

Prepare Your Heart

As our adopted children get older, they may struggle with feeling unwanted and unloved. Even though we, their parents, assure them of our love, they may wrestle with the reality that their birth parents gave them away. There are many ways we can walk alongside our children in this struggle. As we continue to pour out our own love, we can honor their birth parents with our words and talk about them lovingly. We can wonder alongside them about questions we can't answer as we answer the ones we can. But, most importantly, we can point them to God who thought of them first. They were never an accident and were always wanted.

Background

Here, Kaynay lies dreaming about the vastness of space and how God made everything in creation. God is the Creator of the universe, yes – but even more, He is the Creator of your child. He is limited by nothing and created your child with beautiful complexities.

PCR Contemplation

- People often try to put God in a box with ideas of who He is and how He should function. We compartmentalize Him into comfortable sections of our lives or push Him out altogether. How big is God in your life? Is there any area of your heart that you don't want to share with Him?
- Do you realize how deeply God loves you? How intricately He knows you? He sees you at your best and worst and every place in between and loves you more deeply than any other person ever could. Take a moment and ask God what His favorite quality about you is. Be sure to write it down.
- Can we welcome in the wonder and awe of the vastness and simultaneous nearness of God? He is above and beyond all things and yet He chooses to be intimately involved in every detail of our lives. He knows us. He loves us. He delights in us.

Scavenger Hunt
- Can you find the symbol of love? (Answer: The ends of the elephants' trunks and the tips of their tails are all shaped like hearts.)
- How many rabbits are there? (Answer: 4)

Suggested Questions
- Would you rather be a rabbit or an elephant? Why?
- Which rabbit is your favorite?
- What do you think Kaynay is feeling?
     ° How do you think her parents feel?
- Where do you feel the safest?
     ° Follow-up: What things could I do to help you feel safer?

Prepare Your Heart

Time does not contain or limit God – He is utterly beyond it. Although we think about time in a linear way, God sees everything simultaneously and plans everything apart from time.

Also, as you have certainly discovered, adoption of practically every type involves some kind of break, some kind of trauma. God's initial plan was that parents would be married first and then produce children which they would raise in healthy, loving, nurturing homes. However, with the introduction of sin into the world at the Fall in the Garden of Eden, we can see how circumstances occur that don't always fit God's ideal plan. But that doesn't mean things are out of control or that He hasn't provided a way to redeem those circumstances for good.

So, outside of time, God knew and purposed your child. He knew every circumstance of their conception, every beat of their heart. And, in those situations when parenting would not be the best situation for a particular person – for any number of completely valid reasons – He provided a way of redemption which we call adoption.

Background

This scene is still outside of time as we peek into God's thoughts and plans about Kaynay's future adoptive family.

Take note of the adoptive parents' ears. You'll see the dad has checkered ears and the mom has spotted ears. Their coloring is also different from Kaynay. What we wanted to express with the coloring is much more than creativity. We want to show that no matter the color of their skin, they're all elephants. Our daughter doesn't look like either myself or my husband. She clearly didn't emerge from our entwined DNA. We always want to honor her ethnicity, but we never want to idolize ethnic heritage, whether hers or ours. The most important thing to realize is that we're all humans created in the image of our colorful and creative God.

PCR Contemplation

- When God created humanity, because love always has a choice, He gave us free will. Due to our humanity and our inability to be perfect or do purely good, our choices sometimes hurt other people. But God has promised that He will work things out for good for those who love Him and are called by Him (see Romans 8:28). When you look back on your life so far, in what ways do you think God has worked both positive and negative aspects of your life for your good?
- Have any of those ways been surprising or unlikely?
- What areas of your life still await God's redirecting and healing?
- What makes you feel the safest? Why?

The Watering Hole

Scavenger Hunt

- How many animals can you see? (Answer: 8 are visible [including 2 giraffes]; there are 9 total, counting Kaynay in her mother's womb.)
- What similarities do Kaynay and Kaynay's mom have? (Answer: Their coloring along with ear and belly patterns match.)

Suggested Questions

- Would you rather live in water or in the trees?
- What do you think the mama elephant feels knowing a baby is on the way?
- How does God speak? (Answer: God speaks in many ways. Often, He "speaks" however we learn best. If we're more visual, He might put a picture in our mind. If we learn by listening, we might hear an audible Voice or sense a quiet word in our heart. If we're kinesthetic, we might have a gut sense. These are only a few of His unlimited options!)
    - Follow-up: Do you feel like you've ever heard God? How did He "speak" to you?
- What question would you like to ask God right now?

Prepare Your Heart

God spoke! If you go back to Genesis chapter one, you'll see that all of existence came into being when God spoke. Your child began as a thought in God's mind and continues in existence by the voice of God speaking. It's absolutely critical that we as parents help our children learn to hear God's voice, to know that He speaks, and that He hears them. Praying with our children, letting them lead prayer, and practicing times to slow down and listen for God are all powerful opportunities to connect them with their Creator. This, more than any level of education or accomplishment, will set them on a path of purpose and meaning for their life.

Background

- Do you remember taking note of Kaynay's coloring and pink checkered and spotted ears? Meet her birth mom! Standing in the forest, surrounded by the colors and noises and creatures of life, she realizes she's expecting a baby. Over the past several decades, women in the U.S. have had the legal option to end a pregnancy. God has grace, forgiveness, and healing for women who have made that choice. But His ideal is for every child conceived to be given the life He's planned for them. One way we honor our daughter's birth mom is to appreciate the choice she made for life. Despite less-than-perfect circumstances, she made the hard, yet beautiful, choice to give this life a wonderful opportunity.
- Take note of the lion at the water's edge. Following in the footsteps of C. S. Lewis, the famed author of *The Chronicles of Narnia*, the lion here represents Jesus, God's very real and near presence.

PCR Contemplation

- The idea of hearing God has too often been relegated to the super-spiritual and has been understood to only mean an audible Voice. God's ways of speaking are as infinitely creative as He is. Circumstances, the Bible, other people, and peace are a few more ways He speaks.
- Prayer is a two-way street, a dialogue between a person or group of people and God. Speaking and listening. What is your prayer-life like these days? Do you slow down enough to stop and listen?
- As we practice our prayer muscle, it's helpful to confirm that what we're hearing is truly God. Some ways we can do this are confirming with the Bible (because God will not contradict His own nature) and asking a trusted and mature Christian friend to pray about it. When you feel you hear God speak, what do you tend to do?

Scavenger Hunt

- Can you find all of the mushrooms? (There are 12.)
- What's unique about this squirrel? (Answer: Our oldest daughter – age 9 at the time – painted this squirrel on the nursery wall while we prepared for our adopted daughter to arrive. She opted for a two-toned squirrel with a green face and tail on an orange body.)

Suggested Questions

- Would you rather fly like an owl or climb like a squirrel?
- What's inside the mama's belly?
- Where is your favorite place to rest and relax?

Prepare Your Heart

- Our daughter's adoption story has its own messy details, which will remain hers to share as she is led. But one thing we want people to know is that her birth mom made a definitive choice for life. She made one of the hardest decisions we could imagine a mother having to make. And she did it from a heart of love that wanted the best for her daughter. Although this is not always the case, many times it is. And, as adoptive parents, we can be powerful advocates for our children to know that even though messy details exist, the decision for love and life won the day.
- What age-appropriate details about your child's conception and time in utero can you share with them?
- As you discuss this time period, be prepared for your child to experience a wide range of emotions – from curiosity and intrigue to longing and grief.

Background

This scene honors the reality of the mother-child bond during pregnancy. Your adopted child had a beginning before you entered the picture. Here, the mama elephant is taking a bath alongside the river, and we get a peek at the miracle growing within her. While the scene around her is serene, just imagine the turmoil of emotions she's experiencing as she faces a life-altering decision.

PCR Contemplation

- Let's think about your child's birth parents. What do you know about them? Did you have an opportunity to meet them or see pictures? Are they still in your life? How can you bless them and honor them today?
- What's the hardest decision you've ever had to make? What motivated your decision and what made it difficult?
- What assumptions or judgments have you made about others keep you from seeing them as God does? Ask God for His vision and to help you conform your perception of others according to how He sees them.

The Search For Security

Scavenger Hunt
- What is unique about the giraffe in this image? (Answer: He's missing the bottom of his legs. This was not an oversight, but done intentionally to see if anyone would notice.)
- How many hearts can you find in this picture? (Answer: Five – found on three trunks and two tails.)

Suggested Questions
- Would you rather live in the mountains or in the valley? Why?
- What do you know about your birth parents?
    - Follow-up: What do you wish you could know about them?

Prepare Your Heart

One question many children whose parents placed them for adoption ask is: "Why didn't they want me?" They can struggle with the idea that their birth parents rejected them or that they weren't important enough to keep. Birth parents place their children for all kinds of reasons – some thoughtful and loving and others less so. Here, our goal is to help our children see the gift of life their birth parents gave them and seeing that many hearts have been involved in the process, including God's heart. When we choose to view our child's birth parents with empathy and give them the benefit of the doubt, we can help our children establish that mindset as well.

Background

In this image we see Kaynay's mother watching how Kaynay's future adoptive parents interact. Too often birth mothers are considered uncaring or irresponsible, but in reality, they make one of the hardest decisions a mother can make: who is going to take care of their child. As prospective parents, we need to not put our best face on, but be real about how we are going to face challenges and hardships. Often, we (as prospective parents) can be a representation of God's love to these beautiful mothers.

PCR Contemplation

The Lion of Judah makes His second appearance in this book as He guides Kaynay's mother's decision. Know that God knew you would be the parent of your child before the realm of time existed. He knew the challenges you would face, and He knew the celebrations you would get to share. Our hope is that you know how beautiful it is that He chose you to have the honor and responsibility of being a part of your child's life.

We have heard many people say that they could never adopt because they can't control the outcome, but we would challenge that thought. Having a biological child provides no guaranteed results. When we let God take control of our life, we get to be a part of a much larger ministry. We get to let Him control everything and we get to see Him move through us and those around us in ways we could never control or manipulate on our own.

The Hard Waiting

Scavenger Hunt
- What are some ways you see the animals expressing love in this image?
  - Answer: The daddy elephant is sheltering the mommy elephant, the monkey is staying near his friends in their time of need, and most importantly, as parents and friends, they were praying for their little one and their child's birth family.

Suggested Questions
- On a rainy day, would you rather play in the puddles or stay cozy inside?
- What do you think is the hardest part of parenting? (Be ready for varied responses ranging from utterly silly to possibly demeaning. Remember to simply listen to your child's heart in this moment rather than try to correct them.)

Prepare Your Heart

Part of your child's story is how they lived in your heart before they arrived in your home. This mindset and language are vital to regularly express to our children. Be aware, however, of the way you phrase this and how they react. They might interpret your longing for them and your answered prayer as the thing that took them away from their birth parents. Of course, this isn't true, but for a child who may not understand the reasons why their birth parents placed them for adoption, this can be a slippery slope.

Background

We chose a dreary, rainy day as our backdrop for this scene as a reminder of the challenges we face in the waiting. Preparing to adopt a child is no small feat and, often, things don't happen the way we'd hoped, or we face unexpected obstacles. But, even in the challenges and waiting, we can choose where we put our efforts. See the parents on their knees, praying together – and a friend sitting with them nearby. They aren't alone.

PCR Contemplation

Think back to the days, months, perhaps even years that you spent filling out endless paperwork, attending training, raising funds, spreading the word, and perhaps also defending your decision to adopt. Do you remember decorating the room and spending hours in prayer? What obstacles did you face that caught you by surprise? Who stood by you, lending you strength and encouragement? How did that season of work and waiting shape who you are today? What lessons did you take from that time that you now carry as wisdom?

Hope On The Horizon

Scavenger Hunt
- Can you find both celestial bodies in the sky?

Suggested Questions
- Would you rather watch the sunset or the sunrise?
- What do you think your parents thought about you before you came to their family?
    - Follow-up: What do you think they looked forward to while they waited for you?

Prepare Your Heart

As we raise children who came to our families by way of adoption, we must always keep their families of origin in mind. We have our story, and our child has theirs – and our stories intersect when we became a family. We can hold simultaneously the ideas that their birth parent(s) chose life (which was an act of selfless love), that their birth parents felt placing them for adoption was the best choice (for any number of reasons), and that their adoptive parents have loved them before they ever arrived. Prepare yourself for questions throughout the years about your child's birth family and why they chose to place them for adoption. It's inherently messy because imperfect humans (including you) are involved. So we need to take time to consider how we can honor our children's birth parents while providing honest and age-appropriate answers to their questions.

Background

This scene represents the end of a long waiting season for the adoptive parents. We well remember getting the phone call that confirmed our family had been chosen. A birth mother wanted to meet us and see if we were a good fit. All of the emotions swept in: eagerness, hope, anxiety, joy, uncertainty, and more. We had no idea then how everything would turn out, but we couldn't wait to see what came next! The sunrise symbolizes a new beginning, with still more surprises to come. The moon fading in the distance symbolizes the seemingly endless waiting in the dark is coming to an end. The parents stand united, which is critical to maintain through the ups and downs of adoption and parenting.

PCR Contemplation

The adoption process can often feel like a "hurry up and wait" scenario. After the obstacles of paperwork, training, and fundraising have been conquered, there's nothing to do but wait and pray. What was (or is) your waiting process like? Have you experienced fear in the uncertainty? Sometimes it's easy to gloss over difficult emotions we experience with the busyness of adoption, family, and life. It's important to take time to sit with those feelings in God's presence and allow Him to bring healing to soul wounds and help us uproot lies or bitterness that are trying to grow. What emotions do you need to process, as part of your waiting period, that may affect your child's and your family's lives?

If you or your child wants to talk more about God, healing, Jesus or salvation, feel free to reach out to us at life@nowfound.org.

Scavenger Hunt
- Can you find the lone flower?
- Can you spot (pun intended) what is unique about each of the animals?

Suggested Questions
- How do the birth mama and her baby look alike?
    ◦ Follow-up: How is the baby like her adoptive parents?
    ◦ Follow-up: What are your favorite physical features about yourself?
- What do you think the birth mama is feeling?
    ◦ Follow-up: What do you think the adoptive parents are feeling?

Prepare Your Heart

Most privately adopted children had no voice in the circumstances of their adoption. Adults made choices for them, hopefully, in the best interest of the child. Be prepared that your child may experience feelings of frustration, pain, and/or insignificance that they didn't have a choice in the matter. Be prepared that they may wonder how their life might have looked differently if their birth parents had raised them. How can you be ready to receive those frustrations or questions with empathy and compassion?

Background

We see three families in this picture: the elephants in the middle of their adoption; the multi-ethnic jaguar/leopard family, and the giraffes who are currently hoping for a child of their own someday. (See *Loved As You Are* for the giraffes' adoption story.) Families come together in many ways and each one carries its own beauty and challenges. And when our community comes together to celebrate alongside us, family formation through adoption only becomes more beautiful.

PCR Contemplation

We experienced major stepping stones towards our adoption finalization that each held its own sense of awe, joy, and relief. Receiving that first phone call to hear we'd been chosen. Meeting the birth mom. Rooming in at the hospital with our newborn. Signing initial papers after the mandatory 48-hour post-birth period. And, ultimately, finalizing at the courthouse. Every milestone held such weight and value. Looking back at your own journey, what key moments stand out? What myriad of feelings did you experience? How can you share your experiences with your child in age-appropriate ways, so that they can understand that while they may not have had a say in their adoption, their voice carries the power of life and death, everyone experienced pain along the journey, and they are truly significant?

Scavenger Hunt
- How many dots can you find on Kaynay?
  - (Answer: 15, which are visible here on her ear and belly. That may be different from illustrations on other pages.)

Suggested Questions
- What do you think a cloud feels like?
- Would you rather float or be carried?
- Where and when did you begin to exist?

Prepare Your Heart

This entire book emerged as a gift for our adopted daughter – a way to prepare ourselves to answer her deep questions that would surely someday come. We would have pictures and a few short videos of her birth mom, but then nothing as ours is a closed adoption. How would we answer the critical questions...Where did I come from? How did I come to this family? Where did my beginning begin? Prepare yourself for these questions. As you embrace and honor your child's birth family, we also encourage you to live humbly and confidently in your role as their parent.

Background

- The thought of our "beginning" beginning before we existed can be difficult for us to grasp. Most of our memories don't even start until we are a few years old. That is one of the key reasons we want to be sure to impart God's identity into our children. Before they were ever born, they existed as a beloved thought in God's mind. He thought of them first before He knit them together.
- Please note that the color of the skin of God's hand is not white. The historical Jesus was a Middle Eastern Jew. He likely had brown skin and darker hair. We sought to honor that reality in this depiction.

PCR Contemplation

While ours and our children's birthdays are certified and documented, our beginnings actually began well before that date. Some may say that it was about nine months before birth, at the time of conception, which is definitely true of our physical bodies. But even before that moment of new creation, our beginnings began in the mind of our Creator and outside of the realm of time. (To be clear, this is not aligned with the idea of reincarnation where souls are recycled over time. We have a definitive beginning as the Bible clearly states.) Take a moment now and consider how precious each person is – that the God of all creation thought purposefully of each one. He thought of your child uniquely. He thought of you. You have a beginning just like your child – you began in God's own hand.

Dedication

Prepare Your Heart

Having empathy, compassion, and mercy doesn't mean you necessarily condone, endorse, or agree with someone's lifestyle or decisions. Honoring our child's birth parents' choice for life and giving their baby a chance at a life they could not otherwise have is something we can and should all be able to do. As parents, we should all hope to springboard our children forward to new heights beyond what was attainable or available for us. We need to consider these decisions as what they are, likely the easiest and the hardest decision (simultaneously) that anyone could ever make. In the same way, we need to honor our child's birth parents because without them we would not be adoptive parents.

Thank You

Thank you for your part in this beautiful child's life. No matter how small or large your role is in loving this child, it is vitally important to their growth, fulfillment, healing, education, and satisfaction in life. Your prayers, service, generosity, and selfless love for them is not unnoticed and we are so thankful for you.

We hope you and your child enjoy **Where Your Beginning Began** as much as we do. We hope this book helps facilitate many fun and healing conversations with your child as you help them put hope-filled language to their life's story. We are praying for you!

For more resources, including coloring sheets and FAQs about Now Found, please visit http://nowfound.org.

NOW FOUND
PUBLISHING

Visit
Family.NowFound.Org
for more
Land of Fambly
books and additional resources.